COLOUR JETS

KT-399-999

FRANCIS FRY
AND THE O.T.G.

Sam McBratney
& Kim Blundell

Collins

COLOUR JETS

First published in Great Britain by
HarperCollins Publishers Ltd 1996

10 9 8 7 6 5

Text © Sam McBratney 1996
Illustrations © Kim Blundell 1996

The author and illustrator assert the moral right
to be identified as the author and illustrator of the work.

A CIP record for this title is available
from the British Library.

ISBN 0 00 675028-1

Printed in Hong Kong

Chapter 1

Hi. Francis Fry is the name. As you can see from my glass door, I'm a private eye.

Only this morning a lady and her little girl came through that door, and I've been thinking in my swivel chair ever since.

I didn't laugh. I said, "What can I do for you, Madam?"

"Well... we've lost someone awfully precious – haven't we, Elizabeth?" said Mrs Winterspout.

The little girl nodded.

Teddy Brown.

I'm not at my best on Monday mornings, but missing persons are my business.

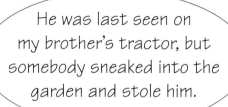

He was last seen on my brother's tractor, but somebody sneaked into the garden and stole him.

And he'd just been to hospital for a new eyeball.

Jumping jackdaws!

Then the truth dawned on me.

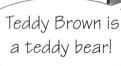

Teddy Brown is a teddy bear!

6

"Of course," said Mrs Winterspout. "And Susan round the corner had her old rocking horse stolen. A whole rocking horse!"

Please say you'll help us, Mr Fry.

Well, the fact is that I don't normally deal in teddy bears and rocking horses. I said I'd think about it and let her know.

That was at ten past nine. Two strong cups of coffee later, the phone rang.

Hello? Is that Francis Fry? This is Elizabeth Winterspout, aged almost eight years old.

I said hello. Then she asked me again if I would look for Teddy Brown – even though she didn't like him very much.

You don't?

Jumping jackdaws! I know somebody
else who doesn't do
that sort of thing.
But he'd like to.
Except the
evening gown.

Think about it.

9

"So why do you want him back?" I asked.

"My mum's awfully upset. Teddy Brown's very old, you know. He used to be Granny's. Please try, Francis Fry."

Does Francis Fry have a heart of stone? How could I refuse?

I'll find Teddy Brown, Elizabeth Winterspout.

Chapter 2

So where do you look for a teddy bear?
Or a rocking horse? I chewed some
liquorice as I strode down the street.

Chewing liquorice helps me think.

Why would anyone steal an old teddy and an ancient rocking horse? Why not steal a computer, or that whizz-kid doll in her flashy car?

Answer: they were both old!

I waved both arms at a passing taxi.

To the Museum of Childhood, please.

The Museum of Childhood was a real eye-opener.

I saw the first pram,

early roller-skates,

and china dolls with fragile faces.

There were slot machines that took big, old-money pennies. And the first edition of the *Beano* –I loved that one!

I was well down memory lane before I remembered what I was there for.

I introduced myself to the assistant.
She had a round face, blunt nose, hair
like a bunch of twigs. No make-up but
painted nails. I study people. In my line
of business this sometimes helps.

That's when she showed me Clarence.
He was a long-snouted bear, the oldest in
the Museum –
maybe the world.

Clarence is worth five or six thousand pounds.

Jumping jackdaws! I wished I was a kid again. I'd keep all my *Beanos*. I'd put my toys in a box and keep them good for forty years.

Think about it.

I walked back to the office. Frankie, I said to myself, this is not some little itty-bitty crime. This is hot stuff. Old toys are big money!

It was time to visit Charlie.

Chapter 3

Charlie is
Chief Inspector at
the local police station.
He was eating lunch at his
computer. Doughnuts and cream.

"Hello Fry," he said. "What's cooking?"

"Very funny, Charlie. Listen, do you
know any bad boys in the antique trade?"

19

When Charlie heard that Teddy Brown was a teddy bear he whipped up his head as if he was a turkey and I'd just mentioned Christmas.

Not the O.T.G. again!

The O.T.G. was news to me.

I watched as Charlie's fingers danced on the computer keyboard:

THE OLD TOY GANG

Thousands of pounds worth
of old toys have been
stolen in recent weeks.
**Thieves to be apprehended
at once.**

Missing items include
  LEAD SOLDIERS
  TEDDY BEARS
  EARLY DINKY CARS
  RUPERT ANNUALS
  DOLLS' HOUSES
  HORNBY TRAINS...

Charlie's swivel chair
squeaked as he spun
to face me.

You see what we're up
against, Frankie? The gang goes in,
gets the old toy, and leaves. Nothing else goes
missing. It's happened all over the city!
How do they know where to go?

I studied the list. It could have been a page from the Museum of Childhood's catalogue. I began to smell a rat. Was Miss Flitt as sweet as she seemed?

Charlie gave me the print-out and I went off to get answers to some questions. Elizabeth Winterspout, aged almost eight years, was depending on me.

It was a long day. First I talked to the owner of Jojo, a bear even older than Teddy Brown.

Finally I came to the last house on the list. A boy came to the door. Freckles. Big teeth. Pale face from watching too much TV.

He certainly was. And so was the whole of the Great Northern Railway. I saw steam locomotives, railway carriages, track, signals, bridges – the works. Even artificial lakes!

Ah, Mr Fry! They stole my Isambard Kingdom Brunel.

Turned out that this was his prize engine.

I made a few notes and left, knowing that I had almost seen a grown man cry. The O.T.G. had to be stopped. Whoever they were.

Chapter 4

I sucked some liquorice and tried to see things clearly. This is what the great detective is always waiting for – that moment when everything becomes clear. You can't rush that moment. It doesn't take orders. You can only revolve in your swivel chair and wait until it happens.

Who… would… know…?

Who would know about Teddy Brown and the rocking horse and Isambard the steam engine and all the other missing ancient toys?

What was the link?

Poor old Jojo, I thought. Imagine having your hip done at his age.

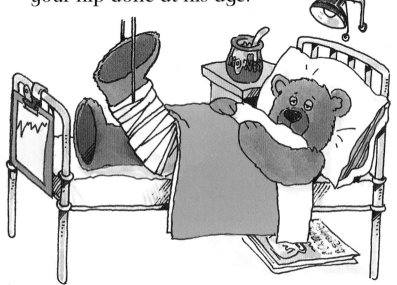

Bang! The moment arrived, a wave of pure light. I stopped revolving, suddenly aware that I knew.

Not who. I didn't know who, not yet. But I knew how.

The new hip-joint.

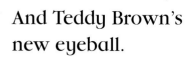

And Teddy Brown's new eyeball.

And Isambard Kingdom Brunel's new paint job.

Think about it.

I walked
my fingers through
the *Yellow Pages.* Bingo!
Then I grabbed my umbrella and hit
the street running.

It was a woman, actually. Susan's mum, Mrs Featheringcoop. Lived round the corner from the Winterspouts.

She said the stolen rocking horse was the first horse ever sat upon by the Duke of Wellington. I looked impressed.

"Well... we had a new tail put on it recently," she admitted. "Real hair from an actual horse, Mr Fry, none of your false rubbish."

Her eyebrows rose like surfacing whales.
"Miss Molly's... but how did you know?"

Because it's my job, I thought as I left.
It's what I'm good at.
Putting two and two
together and
seeing that they
make ten minus
nine plus half
of three times
two.

Think about it.

Chapter 5

Above the shop it said:

I pushed open the door and went in.

Yet another world! Bits of bodies lay everywhere – here an arm, there a leg, over yonder a row of headless dolls. And doll-less heads.

These body-parts shook me up a little. I raised my eyes to the shelves and saw a jar full of black and yellow sweets. Only they weren't sweets. They were eyeballs.

Jumping jackdaws! The fact is, I don't like eyeballs.

What can I do for you, then?

It was Miss Molly herself. She was
stitching leather juggling balls.

On the counter at my elbow
I saw an open copy of the
Museum of Childhood's
catalogue. My heartbeat
quickened when I saw
the name CLARENCE.

Was Little Miss Molly also Big Chief
Number One of the Old Toy Gang?

I decided to test her.

"And how about these?" I said, showing her Charlie's list of missing items.

She recognised them, all right. Suddenly a crafty look came into her eye. "I've never seen 'em things before in my life."

I'd got her! "But Miss Molly, every one of these toys has been to this shop for minor surgery."

Molly barely flinched. She yelled over her shoulder, "HARRY!" and Harry appeared from nowhere.

Jeepers he was big!

Harry walked slowly towards me. Francis Fry, Private Eye was about to be fixed even though he wasn't broken.

They were both crazy! I nipped into a
shop for some
good quality
liquorice.

Molly was right, of course. I had no
proof. They were even after Clarence,
the grand old daddy of them all!
Their party wasn't over.

That gave me an idea.   Party?
No, what we needed was a PICNIC.

Chapter 6

"You're fine,
Charlie," I said,
"you're meant to
look ridiculous."

I was in a mouse suit.
We were both on our way to the
Teddy Bears' Picnic.

This ad had appeared in the local paper:

Teddy Bears' Picnic

Fun for all the family at the Museum of Childhood.

Children - bring your teddies for buns and juice on the lawn.

Mums and Dads - dress up! Be kids again.

See Clarence, the oldest teddy in the country.

Be there. Saturday at 3.00 p.m.

All my idea, of course.
Set a trap. With Clarence as bait.

The Museum wasn't too keen on the idea until we assured them that a force of police officers would be there too, dressed as yellow ducks. If our thieves came down to the woods today, they'd be in for a big surprise.

"It'll never work," said Charlie, rubbing his white kneecaps. They hadn't poked out of short trousers for thirty years.

"It'll work," I said. "Clarence is the honeypot, Charlie. They'll come after him. We can't miss."

The picnic turned out to be more like feeding time at the zoo. You never saw so many bears - short snouts, long snouts, big bears, wee bears, Pooh bears, Rupert bears, even some koala bears.

And not just bears. Pigs, monkeys, giraffes - you name it. Anything that's ever been stuffed was there.

And there was
a hot-air balloon
in the middle of
the garden!

Many of the grown-ups were in fancy
dress. I saw a six-foot chicken waddling
about, and an eighty-year-old Bo Peep
trailing woolly balloons.

Think about it.

Robin Hood was there with his bow and arrows. And a juggling clown.

Juggling balls...
Where had I last seen juggling balls?

It's all going awfully well, Mr Fry. We should have done this years ago!

I smiled, but I was on edge. Any one of these people could be waiting to pounce on the oldest teddy in England.

I turned to Charlie. "Are you sure this garden is sealed off?"

"Frankie, there's no way out. They'll have to fly, old son!"

As all of us must sometimes do, I went to the loo. When I came out and looked at the cradle I nearly wept.

It was empty.

Clarence was gone.

Chapter 7

Jumping jackdaws!
Talk about panic at
the picnic. Miss Flitt
had a fit. Charlie flung
off his wig and blew
his whistle, and a
dozen ducks
ran wild.

But the clown had disappeared. Oh, for a stick of liquorice! Think! Where could he go?

click

Then it came to me. The truth. Not with a blinding light, more of a quiet little click.

Charlie had said it. *"They'll have to fly, old son!"*

But we were too late, the thing was already rising - the six-foot chicken and the juggling clown were waving bye-bye from the basket, and the children were waving back.

Charlie! The hot-air balloon!

59

I was ice cold and deadly calm as I went over to Robin Hood. "May I borrow your bow and arrow, good sir?" I inquired.

I took aim, and let fly. Much depended on that good arrow, and I did not miss

In less than a minute the balloon had
sunk slowly into the next field.

I left the chicken to the ducks and made for the clown.

"Good golly, Miss Molly," I said, "what a time to get a puncture."

Chapter 8

We got everything back.

The Duke of
Wellington's
rocking
horse.

All the teddies.

Even
Isambard
Kingdom
Brunel.

You should have
seen all those people smile.

"I think you must be a very good detective, Francis Fry," said Elizabeth Winterspout, aged almost eight, when Charlie and I brought Teddy Brown home.

I could swear there were tears in Charlie's eyes.